For the shepherd and his lambs –
Flea, Sara and James

First published 1990 by
Walker Books Ltd, 87 Vauxhall Walk, London SE11 5HJ

This edition published 1991

12 14 15 13

© 1990 Kim Lewis

Printed in Hong Kong

British Library Cataloguing in Publication Data
A catalogue record for this book is
available from the British Library.

ISBN 0-7445-1762-1

The Shepherd Boy

Kim Lewis

WALKER BOOKS
AND SUBSIDIARIES
LONDON · BOSTON · SYDNEY

James' father was a shepherd. Every day he got up very early, took his crook and his collie, and went off to see his sheep.

James longed to be a shepherd too.

"You'll have to wait until you're a little older," his father said.

So every day James watched and waited.

James watched and waited all through spring. He watched as the new lambs were born, and saw them grow big and strong.

James watched and waited all through summer. He watched his father clip the sheep, and saw his mother pack the sacks of wool.

James watched and waited all through autumn. He watched his mother help to wean the lambs, and saw his father dip the sheep.

On market-day, James waited while the lambs were sold and heard the farmers talk of winter.

When snow fell, James watched his father feed the hungry sheep near the house, and saw him take hay on the tractor to the sheep on the hill.

Then James waited for his father to come home for tea.

On Christmas Day, James and his father and mother opened their presents under the tree.

James found a crook and a cap and a brand new dog-whistle of his very own.

In a basket in the barn,
James found a collie puppy.
James' father read the card
on the puppy's neck.
It said: *My name is Jess.
I belong to a shepherd boy
called James.*

When spring came
again, James got up very
early. He took his crook
and his cap, and called
Jess with his whistle.

Then James and his
father went off to the
fields together.

MORE WALKER PAPERBACKS
For You to Enjoy

MORAG AND THE LAMB
by Joan Lingard / Patricia Casey

The farmer is concerned that Russell's dog Morag might
worry the sheep – but she ends up saving a lamb!

"A delightful story with true to life illustrations." *Nursery World*

0-7445-2030-4   £4.99

FLOSS
by Kim Lewis

Floss loves playing with the children, but will he make a good sheepdog?

"Kim Lewis draws the British countryside and farm animals
as well as any children's illustrator… A story of warmth and charm …
with a satisfactorily happy ending." *Susan Hill, The Sunday Times*

0-7445-2071-1   £4.99

EMMA'S LAMB
by Kim Lewis

One rainy spring morning, Emma's father brings home a little lost lamb.
He's wet and cold and hungry. Emma wants to keep him and look after him herself.
But in her heart, she knows that Lamb needs to be with his mother.

"Unsentimental and with wonderfully detailed pictures … special."
Valerie Bierman, The Scotsman

0-7445-2031-2   £4.99

Walker Paperbacks are available from most booksellers, or by post from B.B.C.S., P.O. Box 941, Hull, North Humberside HU1 3YQ

24 hour telephone credit card line 01482 224626

To order, send: Title, author, ISBN number and price for each book ordered, your full name and address,
cheque or postal order payable to BBCS for the total amount and allow the following for postage and packing:
UK and BFPO: £1.00 for the first book, and 50p for each additional book to a maximum of £3.50.
Overseas and Eire: £2.00 for the first book, £1.00 for the second and 50p for each additional book.

Prices and availability are subject to change without notice.

2006

THIS WALKER BOOK BELONGS TO:

Archie Mackintosh

Love from

the

'Stewarts'

X

CONTENTS

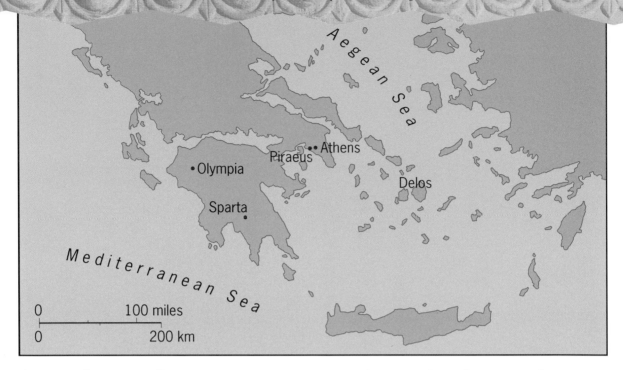

Ancient Greece

Greece is a country that is broken up by mountains and the sea. In ancient times it was very hard to travel around Greece. The Ancient Greeks lived in small groups, around a city. They spoke the same language and had the same religion. But they did not see themselves as Greek. They saw themselves as part of a **city state** (the land controlled by the nearby city). This book looks at how the city states were run and what they were like to live in.

Timeline

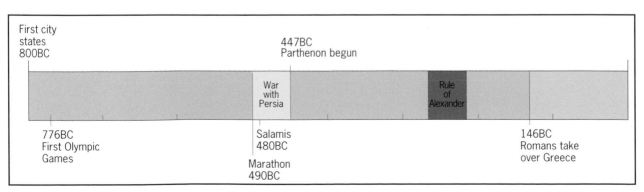

First city
states
800BC

447BC
Parthenon begun

War
with
Persia

Rule
of
Alexander

776BC
First Olympic
Games

Salamis
480BC

Marathon
490BC

146BC
Romans take
over Greece

CITY STATES

What was a city state? It was a city and the farming land around it. Some city states were very small and could have less than a thousand **citizens**. The biggest and most powerful city states were Athens and Sparta. They had several thousand citizens.

ARISTOTLE, THE ATHENIAN PHILOSOPHER (THINKER), WROTE THAT THE SIZE OF A CITY STATE WAS IMPORTANT:

You can't have a state of ten citizens. But when you have 100,000 it is no longer a city state. It has to be big enough to run itself. But it has to be small enough for the citizens to know each other. Otherwise how can they choose officials?

This photo shows Athens from the air. You can see the Parthenon, with its strong walls, on the right.

City states were run in different ways. Some of them were run by kings. Others were run by a small group of powerful men (who came from rich and important families in the city). Other city states, like Athens, were run by all the **citizens**. Not everyone in Athens had a say in what went on. You had to be a citizen to take part.

ATHENIAN CITIZENS

A citizen had to be a man. He had to be free, and not a slave. He had to be the son of an Athenian citizen. He had to be over 17 years old. Less than a third of the people of Athens took part in making the decisions.

ALL THE SAME?

Although city states were run in different ways, they all had similar ideas about which people were the most important. **Slaves** were the least important. The most important were rich male citizens. Even in Athens, these were the people most likely to make the decisions. Then came other male citizens. Then came women, children and foreigners. Women and men lived almost separate lives. Women stayed at home most of the time, in a separate part of the house. They went out as little as possible.

A city **agora**

Athens started as a small **city state**. It grew to become one of the biggest and most powerful. As it grew, the city became more important and the countryside around became less so. Athens had too many people to feed them from food grown in the farmland around. So Athens had to **trade goods**, like pottery and statues, with other countries or Greek **colonies** for food. Athens was near the sea, but not beside it. As it grew and traded more and more, the nearby **port** of Piraeus became big and important too.

People voted on decisions by raising their hands. When more careful counts were needed **ballots** were used. These ballots were used by people in trials to say if they thought the accused person was guilty or not.

VOTING

Athens was a **democracy** in which all **citizens** voted. Meetings were held about 40 times a year at the Pnyx, a hill near the city. Citizens were rounded up by men with ropes to make sure that they went! A list of things to decide was read out. Citizens spoke if they wanted, and then they all voted.

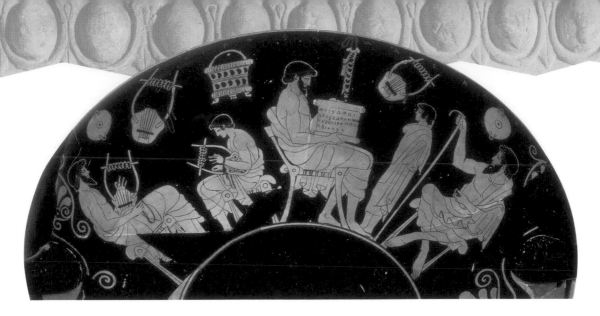

EDUCATION

Education was important in Athens. A good speaker could affect decision making. Boys went to school to learn to read, write and make speeches. They read books and plays. Many Athenians thought that being a good speaker and thinker was very important — even more important than being a good soldier or hard worker.

Boys went to school for part of the day. They also went to wrestling school, so that they were fit when they began to train as soldiers. All men were expected to fight for their city state.

A GREEK WRITER, CALLED PLATO, DESCRIBED SCHOOLS IN ATHENS IN ABOUT 390BC:

As soon as boys know their letters and can read well, their teachers give them the works of good poets to read and learn to set the boys a good example of how to behave. Boys also go to wrestling school, so they are fit and able to be brave when they go to war. Sons of wealthy parents begin school at the earliest age and finish their schooling the latest.

Sparta was a very different **city state** from Athens. They had both begun in a similar way: they had been ruled by kings. Athens went on to have a **democracy**. Sparta was ruled by two kings and a **council** of important men who ran everything.

SPARTAN IDEAS

The most important thing for a Spartan man was to be a good soldier. They trained for this from birth. In Sparta, officials decided whether to let new-born babies live. They chose only the strongest boys and girls. When a boy was seven he left home to be brought up with other boys. He lived with other soldiers until he was 30. If he married, he had a house for his wife and visited from time to time. After he became 30 he could live at home.

PLUTARCH, A WRITER, DESCRIBED SCHOOLS IN SPARTA:

They learned reading and writing for basic needs, but the rest of their education was to make them brave, well-disciplined soldiers. Their bodies were tough, unused to baths and lotions.

SPARTAN WOMEN

Spartan girls were expected to be very fit, unlike girls in other city states. The usual women's jobs of spinning and weaving were considered to be not active enough for Spartan women. They were encouraged to be active and healthy so that they would have strong, healthy babies.

A bronze figure of a Spartan girl running.

Many important thinkers were Greek. Some of their ideas are still talked about now. Most of them believed that thinking ideas through and proving them was enough. Only a few of them made useful inventions, one of these was Archimedes. He is interesting because he was so unusual.

ARCHIMEDES

Archimedes was born in about 287BC. He invented a way of lifting water from rivers, so that it could be used to water farmland. He worked out that by using a lever which was properly balanced you could move very heavy loads. He proved it by **launching** the biggest ship he could find, the *Syracusa*. It was fully loaded and weighed about 1800 tonnes. By using a complicated system of levers and pulleys, Archimedes launched it from a ramp all by himself.

Archimedes designed several weapons to help the Greeks to fight the Romans. He was killed in 212BC, when the Romans captured his city. There is a story that he was killed by a Roman soldier for refusing to be arrested until he had finished an experiment he was working on!

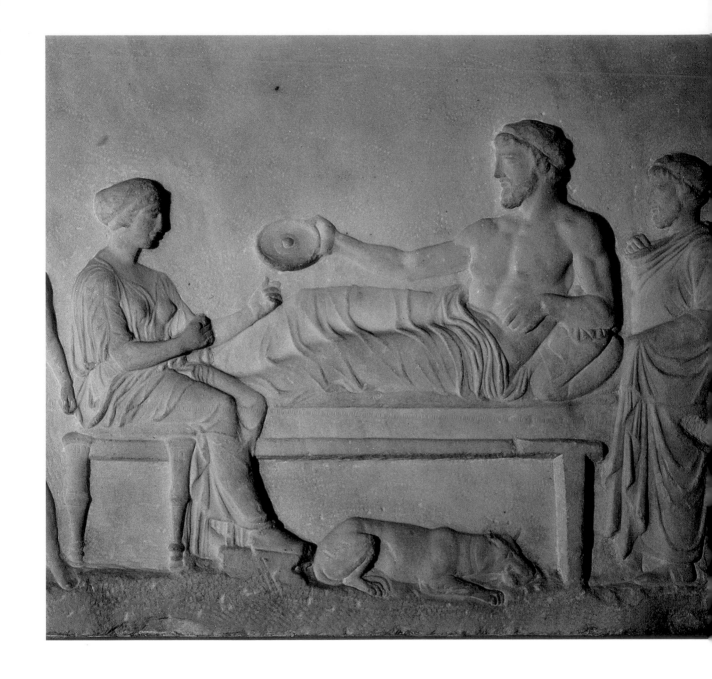

People disapproved of some thinkers. One example is
Socrates, who taught young men to question their
elders. He was accused of corrupting the young men,
and was sentenced to death. This frieze shows him
drinking the poisoned wine given to kill him.

Writing was important to the Ancient Greeks. Even the Spartans believed that everyone needed to learn to read and write. Much of what we know about the Greeks, we know because of the books and plays they wrote. Many of these have survived and we can read them today.

THE ALPHABET

Our word 'alphabet' comes from the first two letters of the Greek alphabet, 'alpha' and 'beta'. Our alphabet has been worked out from the Greek one. We do not share all the letters of the alphabet, because English does not make the same sounds as Greek.

WHAT DID THEY WRITE ON?

The earliest Greeks carved writing on to stones, or scratched it on to metal or pieces of pottery. Boys practised writing at school on wax, so mistakes could be smoothed out. Later, they used paper scrolls and books. The paper was made from the stalks of papyrus reeds. Most of the paper came from Egypt.

This example of Greek writing, dating from before 500BC, was scratched on to lead, which could be used because it is a reasonably soft metal.

Temples were the grandest and most important parts of any city. They were also the best built. They are the buildings most likely to have survived until now. A temple was the home of the god or goddess it was dedicated to. Only **priests** and **priestesses** could go into a temple. Ordinary people did not go inside. The **religious ceremonies** and the **sacrifices** were held outside.

PRIESTS AND PRIESTESSES

Priests and priestesses were important people. They ran the temples and made the sacrifices to the many gods and goddesses of Ancient Greece. The Greeks believed in many different gods and goddesses who could come to earth and interfere in the lives of ordinary people. So the gods had to be kept happy with prayers, sacrifices and religious ceremonies. Greeks believed their gods and goddesses behaved like people and could get into fights, fall in love and become jealous. People could pray to the gods at home, but they also had to go to the temples for the big religious ceremonies.

A procession to a temple.

Almost every Greek city had at least one theatre. Many of them have survived, so people are able to study them today. Theatre performances were part of **religious ceremonies**. They only happened a few times in a year. You could not go to the theatre every day.

The playwrights who wrote the plays used stories that people knew. They did not make up new stories. Many plays were written specially for a ceremony. Three were chosen and performed. The audiences voted for the one they liked best.

WHO ACTED?

All the actors were men. Because they were a long way from many of the people in the audience, the actors wore heavy masks made of linen, cork or wood. These masks clearly showed the audience what the actor was supposed to be – a man or a woman, young or old. Some masks had a happy face on one side and a sad one on the other, so an actor could change his feelings by turning the mask around.

The Greek theatre at Syracuse in Sicily.

WHO WENT?

Men wrote plays and went to the theatre. Some historians think women did not go to the theatre because they had to stay at home, keeping away from the men. Other historians say that women went to **religious festivals**, and plays were part of these, so they may have gone to the theatre. We have no proof either way.

As plays became more complicated, two kinds developed. Tragedies re-told myths, which were usually stories in which the most important character has an unhappy end. They warned against arguing with the gods, or getting too proud or important. Comedies were funny. They made fun of all sorts of people. Their characters and story-lines were more ordinary. They were often rude, as well as funny. There were often dwarfs in the comedies, acting as servants. They were the earliest sort of circus clown.

MENANDER

A playwright called Menander was born in about 341 BC. He lived in Athens and came from an important family. He wrote mostly comedies. His plays won first prize several times. Only one whole play has survived. We know he wrote over a hundred plays because other writers talk about them in their plays and books. He died in about 291 BC.

A carving of Menander looking at actors' masks. He is holding a mask of a young man. On the table beside him are masks for an older man and a woman.

ACTORS

What do we know about Ancient Greek actors? Some actors became well known as tragic or comic actors. But they were not famous in the way actors are now. Firstly, no one saw their faces. They wore masks to act. Secondly, they only acted when there was a **religious festival**. Thirdly, the playwright and his ideas were what was seen as important, not the actors.

THE CHORUS

Plays were either spoken or sung, in rhyme. The actors stood on a stage behind the **orchestra**. The orchestra was not the musicians! It was a big space in the centre of the theatre where the chorus stood. There were about fifteen people in the chorus. They all spoke together. They told the story and made comments on what was happening. They also danced and sang. The actors got the big speeches. Only three actors were on the stage at any time. But they could play more than one part.

A play being performed in a Greek theatre. The chorus are in the orchestra on the right.

The Ancient Greeks held the first Olympic Games. All the **city states** in Greece joined in. If any of them were fighting each other, they stopped to let each other travel to get to the Olympics. The Olympics were held every four years like they are now. But they were different in several ways.

A RELIGIOUS FESTIVAL

The Olympics were part of a **religious festival** held at Olympia. It was held in honour of the most important of the gods, Zeus. They began with religious **processions** and **sacrifices**. Two and a half of the five days of the Olympics were taken up with **religious ceremonies**.

MEN ONLY

Only men could take part in the Olympics. The athletes competed naked. Women could not watch. The punishment for women caught watching was to be thrown off a cliff! Women had their own Games, which were held at the same time but in a different part of Olympia. They were held in honour of Zeus' wife, Hera.

A race at the Olympics. Running is one of the events that is still part of today's Olympic Games.

Aren't you burned by the sun? Aren't you crowded and tight-packed? Aren't the washing facilities bad? Aren't you soaked to the skin when it rains? Don't you get more than enough noise and shouting and other unpleasantness? Yet you put up with all this because it is such a marvellous spectacle.

All Greeks were expected to keep fit, not just athletes. **City states** could call on their people to fight at any time. So keeping fit was important in case you had to go to war. Doctors said keeping fit kept you healthy. All Greek towns had at least one **gymnasium** – a place where men could go to exercise.

AT THE GYMNASIUM

A gymnasium was not a building, as it is now. It was an open park with trees and grass. There were running tracks marked out, and sandy areas for jumping, boxing and wrestling. There were also changing rooms and places to wash.

NOT JUST EXERCISE

Men went to a gymnasium to chat, not just to exercise. In Athens' gymnasium a lot of teaching went on too. Famous thinkers taught small groups. By 250BC some gymnasiums even had libraries and lecture rooms.

EVIDENCE FROM THE TIME

We know about the important buildings, like **temples**, in cities because they have survived and can be studied.

NEW EVIDENCE

Archaeologists have excavated parts of some Greek cities. There is not much left to study. Ordinary houses, made from mud brick, have crumbled away. Also, some cities, like Athens, have been lived in ever since ancient times. Modern homes cover the ancient city.

A DESCRIPTION OF ATHENS, WRITTEN IN ABOUT 320BC:

The city is dry and dusty, with a bad water supply. The streets are badly planned, because the city is so old. Many of the houses need repairs, and there are not many large ones. A stranger would be very surprised that this was the famous city of Athens. But the public buildings are magnificent. The theatre is large and beautiful. The Temple to Athena, called the Parthenon, is clearly visible from a long way off. Anyone who sees it will be amazed by it.

The Kew Gardens
WORLD OF FLOWERS
COLOURING BOOK

*Over 40 beautiful illustrations
plus colour guides*

ARCTURUS

ROYAL BOTANIC GARDENS

All illustrations included in this book have been taken from the Library, Art & Archives Collections of the Royal Botanic Gardens, Kew.

Special thanks to everyone at Kew Publishing, Lynn Parker, Art and Illustrations Curator, and Dr Martyn Rix, Editor of *Curtis's Botanical Magazine*.

ARCTURUS

This edition published in 2016 by Arcturus Publishing Limited
26/27 Bickels Yard, 151–153 Bermondsey Street,
London SE1 3HA

ISBN: 978-1-78428-322-3
CH005242NT
Supplier 37, Date 0916, Print run 5561

Printed in Romania

Created for children 10+